On the Edge

It's My Business

Mary Green

United Kingdom: Folens Publishers, Apex Business Centre, Boscombe
Road, Dunstable, LU5 4RL.
Email: folens@folens.com

Ireland: Folens Publishers, Greenhills Road, Tallaght, Dublin 24.
Email: info@folens.ie

Poland: JUKA, ul. Renesansowa 38, Warsaw 01-905.

Editor: Kay Macmullan
Layout artist: Lee Williams
Cover design: Duncan McTeer
Illustrations: Josephine Blake

First published 2003 by Folens Limited.

© 2003 Folens Limited, on behalf of the author.

British Library Cataloguing in Publication Data. A catalogue record for
this publication is available from the British Library.

ISBN 1 84303 384–4

Contents

The story so far

If you haven't read an *On the edge* book before:
The stories take place in and around a row of shops and buildings called Pier Parade in Brightsea, right next to the sea. There's Big Fry, the fish and chip shop; Drop Zone, the drop-in centre for local teenagers; Macmillan's, the sweet and souvenir shop; Anglers' Haven, the fishing tackle shop; the Surf 'n' Skate shop and, of course, the Brightsea Beach Bar.

If you have read an *On the edge* book you may have met some of these people before.

Em Mistry: *lives with her mum, her father left a few years ago. Best friends with Jan.*

Yasmin Mistry: *has brought up her daugher, Em, by herself since her husband, Ravi, left.*

Jan Macmillan: *Em's best friend, Jan works for her mum in the sweet and souvenir shop during the holidays.*

So, what's been going on?
Em has been living alone with her mum, Yasmin, ever since her father walked out on them. Mrs Mistry is naturally very protective, but she knows she can't control Em's life completely. Fortunately, there is one person Em can tell her business to – her best friend, Jan.

What happens in this story?
Em's mum makes her promise not to go down to the storm-damaged Pier Parade, but Em disobeys. What she finds there has nothing to do with the storm, but it still creates havoc in her life.

1

It's so unfair!

"Everyone's talking about the storm. It came out of the blue yesterday, you know. Just like that. Part of the old pier came down. And some of the shops in Pier Parade were smashed."

Em was in the kitchen with her mum, Yasmin.

Suddenly she stopped talking.

She turned up the radio.
"A wall of water swept over Pier Parade. The worst gales since …"

"Listen to that!" said Em. "I'm meeting Jan. We're gonna help. Her mum's shop was hit."

"I don't want you going anywhere near the parade today, Em," her mum said.

Em stopped.
"Why?" she said.

"Because I don't."

"But why?"

"Because I *don't*."

"Jan'll be there. They all will. They're all going to be there."

"Now listen to me, Em. I don't want you anywhere near Pier Parade. Do you *understand* me?"

"But …"

"That's quite enough! No more talk!" Her mum was almost shouting now.

Em pushed back her chair and got up.
She never had moods.
But she was in a mood now.
It was so unfair!

She went into her room, slamming the
door behind her.
She waited for her mum to react.

Nothing happened.

What was the matter with her mum?
Why was she so mean today?
It wasn't like her.

They got on well most of the time.
But she was laying down the law now
all right.

What could Em do?

She wanted to go to Pier Parade.
She wanted to meet her friends.
She didn't want to be left out.

But she couldn't just walk off.
She couldn't defy her mum straight to
her face.

She looked at her watch.
It was 12 o'clock.
They were all going to meet at 12.30.
She had to leave soon or she would
miss them.

She would have to phone Jan.

She found her mobile and rang her friend.

'Call failed' came up on the screen.

Well, she could text her.
She sent a simple message.

Where R U?

She waited.
And waited.

Nothing.

She sent a new message, spelling out the words.

Where are you? Text me NOW!

'Call failed' she read.

Em flung the mobile on to the chair.

2

Pancakes

It was 1 pm.

Em was still in her room.
Her mum was still in the kitchen.

Jan had still not rung.
It was hopeless!

Em was fed-up, really fed-up.
She was staring out of the window when
there was a knock at her bedroom door.

Em didn't respond.

There was another knock.

"Open the door, Em. Let's talk about this."

"It's too late now!" shouted Em. "I hope you're happy."

Slowly the door began to open.
Em didn't turn round.

Her mum came in and closed the door quietly.

"I'm sorry, Em," her mum began, "but I don't think it's a good idea for you to go to the parade today."

"I know that! Is that all you've come to tell me?"

"I don't think it's a good idea, because it's not safe. And I don't want you to get into trouble."

"What? Don't be daft. I'll be with Jan's mum!"

What was her mum talking about?

"When it's safe, we'll go down together. We could go down on Saturday. We could help Jan's mum then."

"Go down together? I'm not a baby!"

Her mum sighed.

"I have to visit Auntie Mina in half an hour. D'you want to come?"

"No!" said Em.

"OK, but when I've gone, I don't want you sneaking off. Do you understand?"

Em didn't reply.

"Em? Do you understand?"

"Mmm," she said under her breath.

"I've made some pancakes for you. They're in the kitchen."

"Pancakes! Huh! Who wants pancakes?" moaned Em.

3

Plotting

When her mum had gone, Em didn't
do anything.
What could she do?
Her mum would kill her if she went
out now.

She got up and went into the kitchen.
The pancakes were there.
A bit cold, but still tasty.

There were four.
She ate them all.

Two with tomato and cheese.
Two with lemon and honey.

When she had finished she felt better and
she began to think.

Her mum was very odd today.
Why was she so against her going to
the parade?
She knew she would be with Jan's mum.
And what did she mean about getting
into trouble?

It didn't ring true, somehow.

The more Em thought about it, the odder
it seemed.
And the more unfair it seemed, too.
And if it was unfair, why shouldn't
she go?

Em began to plot.

She knew she shouldn't go.
But if she *did* go, she would have to do it
without her mum finding out.

Then she had a brainwave!

She could ring her mum.
And say she had changed her mind about
meeting Auntie Mina.

She would meet up with them, but go by Pier Parade on the way.

Brilliant!

It might take a little time, but it could work.

Her mum would never know!

And it would only be half-wrong, wouldn't it?

4

A strange meeting

"Well, if I meet you at the park entrance in an hour, will that be OK?"

Her mum seemed pleased.
Em switched off her mobile.

Then she grabbed her bag and her jacket.
She ran down the stairs and out of
the flat.

When she got to the top of the street she
was still running.

To get to the park she would have to
turn right.
Instead, she turned left towards
Pier Parade.

When she saw the seafront she
was shocked.

What a mess!
It looked like a bombsite.
There were broken bricks and tiles on
the ground.
There was glass and bits of metal.
And there were shells, pebbles and
driftwood from the sea.

The police were further along.
There was a barrier to keep the
public away.

Em looked around to see if she could
find Jan.

There was no sign of her.
And she couldn't see her other
friends either.

She walked along in the direction of Pier
Parade but she only got so far.

A burly policeman came up to her.
"And where d'you think you're going,
young lady?"

"I have to get to the parade. My friend's
down there. Her mum's shop has been
hit and … "

The policeman cut in.
"Well, there's nobody down there now.
The shop owners have been sent away for
the present. It's unsafe. So, I don't think
you can be much help, can you, Miss?"

"Oh," said Em. "So I can't go
down there?"

"That's right. Got it in one."

He was still blocking her path.
He didn't look as if he was going to shift.
So Em had no choice.
She turned and walked back the way she
had come.

"Well that was a dead loss," she said
to herself.

She looked at her watch.
She had twenty minutes before setting off
to meet her mum and Auntie Mina.

As she walked up the path, thinking
about what to do, she saw a woman
ahead of her.

She didn't think much about it at first.
Then she noticed that there was a man
with her.
He was walking in front, holding the
hand of a small child.

He turned around to speak to the woman
and Em stopped in her tracks.

She couldn't believe what she saw.
She stared.
She gasped.
She felt hot then cold.
She wanted to run away.
But her feet were rooted to the spot.

It was him!

And he was looking at her.

Em could see that the same panic had taken hold of him.

"What is it, Ravi?" the woman asked. "You look as if you've seen a ghost?"

"I have," he said.

Beads of sweat were breaking out on his forehead. He brushed his black hair to one side.

The last time Em had seen him they had gone out for the day, to the funfair. There had been candyfloss and dodgems. She couldn't remember much more. But it had been a good day.

Then he had gone.

This was the first time she had seen him in three years.

He was the first to break the silence. "Em? It is you, isn't it?"

All she could say was one simple word: "Dad."

5

Where's Em?

"If that girl doesn't turn up soon, I'm going down to the parade."

"The best thing to do is to stay here, Yasmin ... and calm down," said Mina.

They were waiting at the park entrance.

Em was twenty-five minutes late and there was no sign of her.

"If she's gone down to the parade, when I told her not to, there'll be hell to pay, that's all! You know why I don't want her to go."

Mina sighed.
"Yes, I know why. But what can you do? She's growing up and young people aren't what they were. You have to change with them."

Em's mum raised her eyebrows.
This was new, coming from Mina.

"Well, I'm not going to talk about all that now, I just ..." she began. "Look! There she is!"

They both started waving.

"And don't be too hard on her," said Mina quietly.

Em came running up.

"Where have you been? You're half an hour late," said her mum.

"I ... I left the house late," Em said.

Her mum looked at her closely.
There was something not right.
Em looked shocked and upset, as if she'd been crying.
She decided to say nothing for the moment.

"Let's go and have some ice-cream," she said. "And I bet Mina could murder a cup of tea."

They walked into the park and over to the open-air café.
Em and Mina sat down at a table while Em's mum went to get the ice-cream.

"What's up, then?" said her auntie.

Em bit her lip.
"It's bad," she said. "Really bad."

"You'd better tell me then."

Em told her everything.

How she had met her dad and his new partner.
And how she had found out that she had a little half-brother.
How she had wanted to run away, but had cried instead.

And then how … she paused at this point, took a deep breath and said, "I'm going to meet up with him again. But don't say anything to Mum, will you?"

"She'll have to know sometime," said Mina.

"Yes, but not yet. Not yet," pleaded Em.

6

It all comes out

"What happened, Em? Why *were* you late?"

Em was sitting at the kitchen table. She was playing with the sugar.

Her mum came and sat down.

"You don't fool me, you know. You went to Pier Parade, didn't you? That's what all this is about."

Em looked up and bit her lip.

She didn't know what to say. She didn't know where to begin.

"Sort of," she said.

"What do you mean, 'sort of'?"

"Well, I did. Yes. On my way to meet you. But I couldn't get through. The police were there. And I couldn't see Jan or anyone else so I … I left."

"And that made you half an hour late?"

"It took ages to get to the park because …"

Em stopped.

She couldn't think of a reason.

So she looked at the table and said quietly, "I bumped into Dad."

Em waited, but her mum said nothing. She just put her head in her hands.

This made Em feel worse not better.

Her mum looked up slowly.
"Where? How?" she said.

Em explained.
"And, Mum, he's got another woman …
and a little boy, my brother."

Her mum sighed, but didn't
look shocked.
"I know," she said.

Now it was Em's turn to ask questions.

"You knew! So why didn't you tell me?"

"Lots of reasons. You know how the
family were when he left. We couldn't
talk about him. And when I found out, I
didn't want to upset you."

"Did Auntie know?"

"Yes, I told her."

"But you didn't tell me?"

"No one else knows, Em. I thought it best if you didn't."

Em's mind was racing.

"And did you know he'd be around Pier Parade? Was that why you were so funny this morning?"

"He still has property there. He doesn't visit it very often. But I thought he might after the storm. And I didn't want any trouble."

"What's going on? What else don't I know?"

"Nothing, Em. That's it."

Em stood up.
"That isn't it!" she said. "I'm going to see him again and you can't stop me."

Her mum looked hurt.

"Em, think carefully before …"

But Em broke in.

"It's my business. You can't stop me."

7

Talking to Jan

"Well, I think you're mad," said Jan.

"Why? He is my dad," said Em.

"Some dad," said Jan. "He didn't bother with you. Why bother with him?"

Jan wasn't thinking about Em's feelings.
But Em didn't mind.
She wanted an honest point of view about meeting up with her dad again.

"But, if it was your dad, you would."

"I don't know if I would," said Jan. "I hardly see him anyway. He's always off in that lorry."

"Doesn't your mum mind?"

"Dunno. Don't think so. He gets under her feet when he's at home, she says."

Then she added, "He's all right for a laugh sometimes. And he gives me money when he comes back. But that's about it."

"Well, there's my little brother," said Em, getting back to the point.

"Mmm," said Jan. "If you want to see him, you'll have to see your dad."

"The only real problem is I feel sorry for my mum," said Em. "I know she should have told me, but she only did it to … kind of … protect me. And now she's got to meet him again. And she doesn't want to."

"She doesn't have to," said Jan.

"She says if I'm going to see him, she wants to meet him first to tell him a few things."

"Well, if she wants to tell him a few things, she'll have to see him," said Jan.

8

Talking to Ravi

Yasmin and Ravi were sitting in the open-air café in the park.

It was not an easy meeting.
Yasmin was angry.
She wanted answers.
Ravi felt uncomfortable.

"I didn't want to upset anyone. So I kept away," he said.

"Upset anyone? Upset anyone? She's your daughter! And what about your family, your mother and father?"

"It just seemed better that way," he said.

"Have you any idea what it's been like?"

"Well, I send you money every month."

"And so you should. As I said, she's your daughter. But it's not only about money. I'm raising her on my own. And now you bump into her and think everything can be all right again."

"I know things are different. But I'd like to make amends. See her. Take her out."

"You can never make amends to me, or her. You've lost three years of her life."

But Ravi carried on, not listening.
"I could take her out somewhere with little Sanj. She'd like him. Think about it. Will you?"

Em's mum sighed.
She was more sad than angry now.
And she was fed up with rows.

"Perhaps I should have told her everything," she said. "But I was only trying to protect her. I can't forgive you, Ravi. And I don't like the idea of Em having anything to do with you. But it's not up to me anymore."

She added, "It's up to Em. Even Mina thinks that."

9

New beginning?

So every fortnight Em did meet her dad and Sanj.

They came to the flat to collect her.

Ravi never came in, but sometimes he met Yasmin on the doorstep and there were no rows.

As Em said to Jan a few months later, "Once, I hoped they'd get back together, my mum and dad. I even used to dream about it. Then I knew it was hopeless and I thought I'd never see my dad again. But that seems a long time ago. Funny how things turn out, isn't it?"

"Yeah. Dead funny," said Jan.

Then she added, "But parents, they give you grief. They're all a pain in the neck, one way or another, if you ask me."